TEEN TITANS GO!™

Little, Brown and Company

Hachette Book Group
1290 Avenue of the Americas, New York, NY 10104
Visit us at lb-kids.com

Little, Brown and Company is a division of Hachette Book Group, Inc.
The Little, Brown name and logo are trademarks of Hachette Book Group, Inc.

The publisher is not responsible for websites (or their content) that are not owned by the publisher.

First Edition: April 2015

Library of Congress Cataloging-in-Publication Data

Belle, Magnolia.
Chillin' like a villain / adapted by Magnolia Belle. — First edition.
    pages cm
"Teen Titans go!"
"Based on the episode 'Starfire the Terrible' written by Steve Borst."
Summary: When Robin, the leader of the Teen Titans, needs an archenemy, his teammate Starfire generously offers to fill in the role, and she far exceeds Robin's expectations.
ISBN 978-0-316-33329-0 (trade pbk.)
[1. Superheroes—Fiction. 2. Supervillains—Fiction.] I. Borst, Steve.
II. Teen Titans go! (Television program) III. Title.
PZ7.B4144Ch 2015
[E]—dc23   2014040290

10 9 8 7 6 5 4 3

CW

Printed in the United States of America

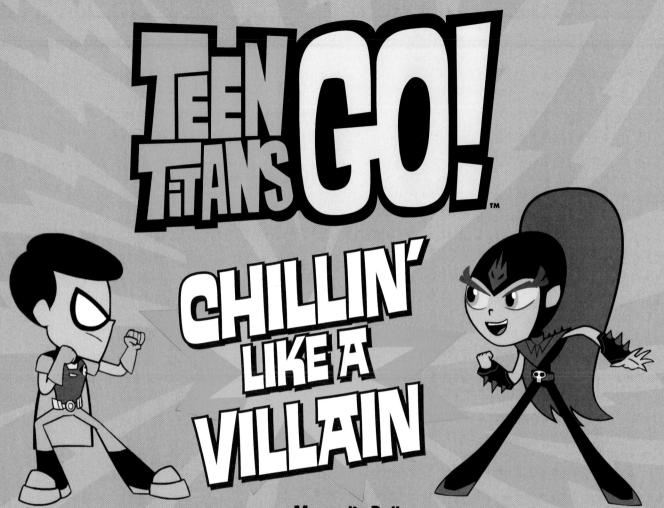

TEEN TITANS GO!™

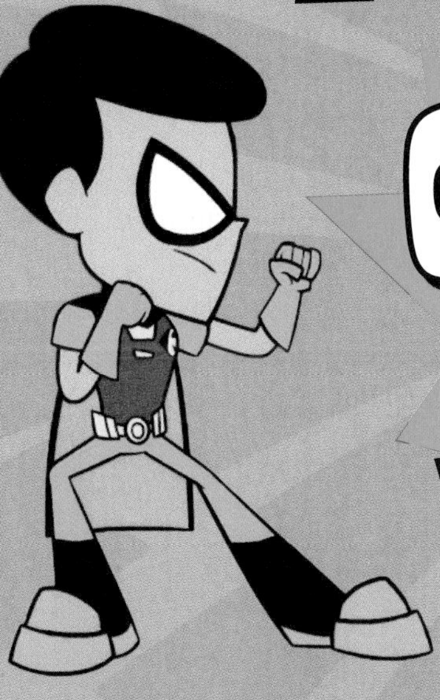

CHILLIN' LIKE A VILLAIN

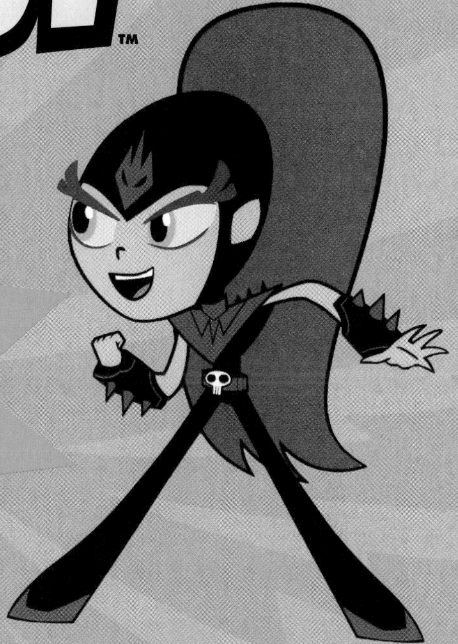

Adapted by Magnolia Belle

Based on the episode "Starfire the Terrible"

written by Steve Borst

LB

LITTLE, BROWN AND COMPANY

New York Boston

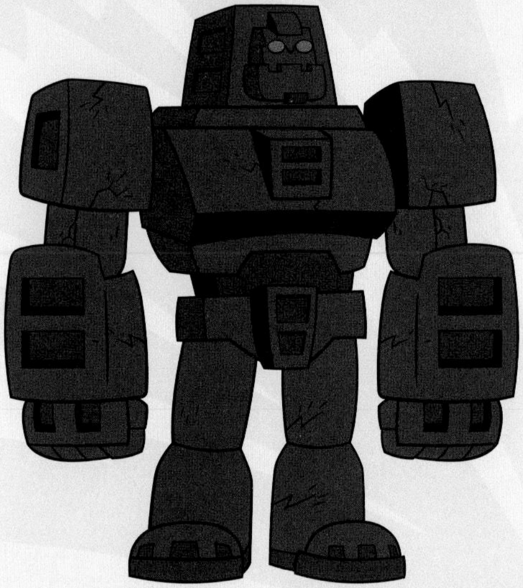

The Teen Titans are on patrol when they spot the monstrous villain Cinderblock. He causes a real ruckus at the railroad yard, but the Titans just stand by and watch as he destroys all the trains!

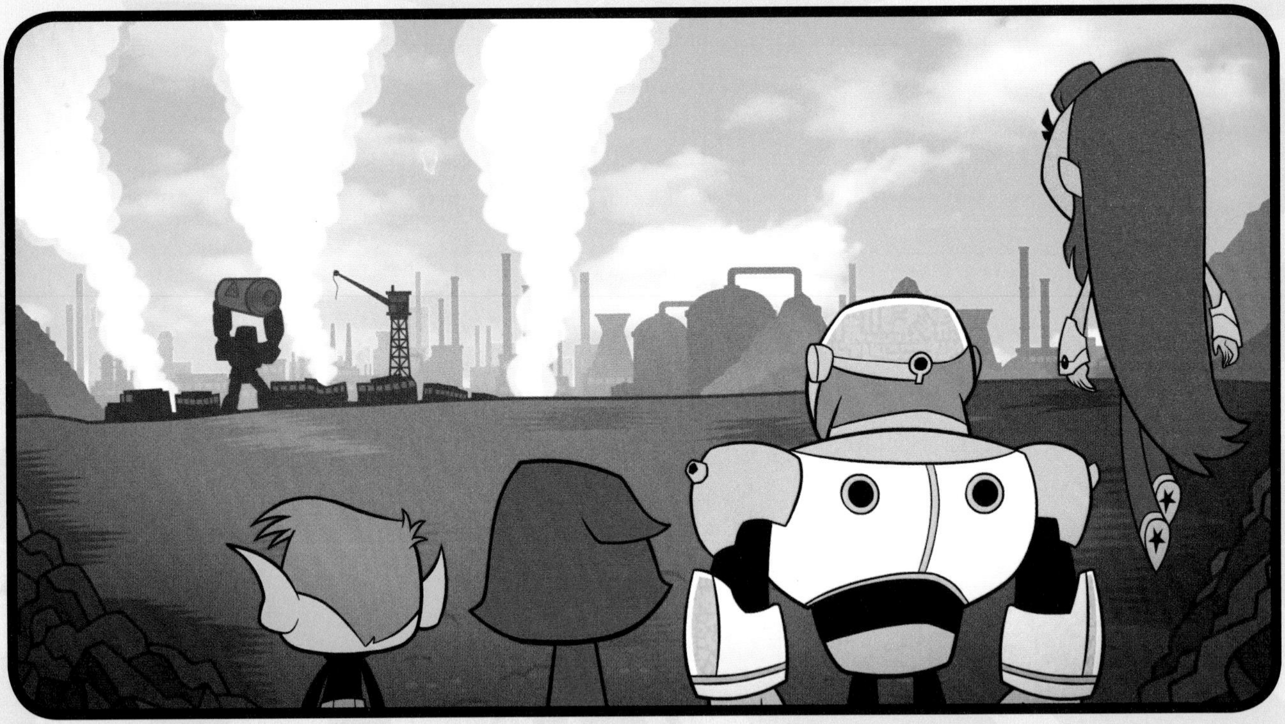

"Soooo, shouldn't we do something about Cinderblock?" Raven asks.

Cyborg sighs and replies, "We can't. Today is Monday. You know what that means...."

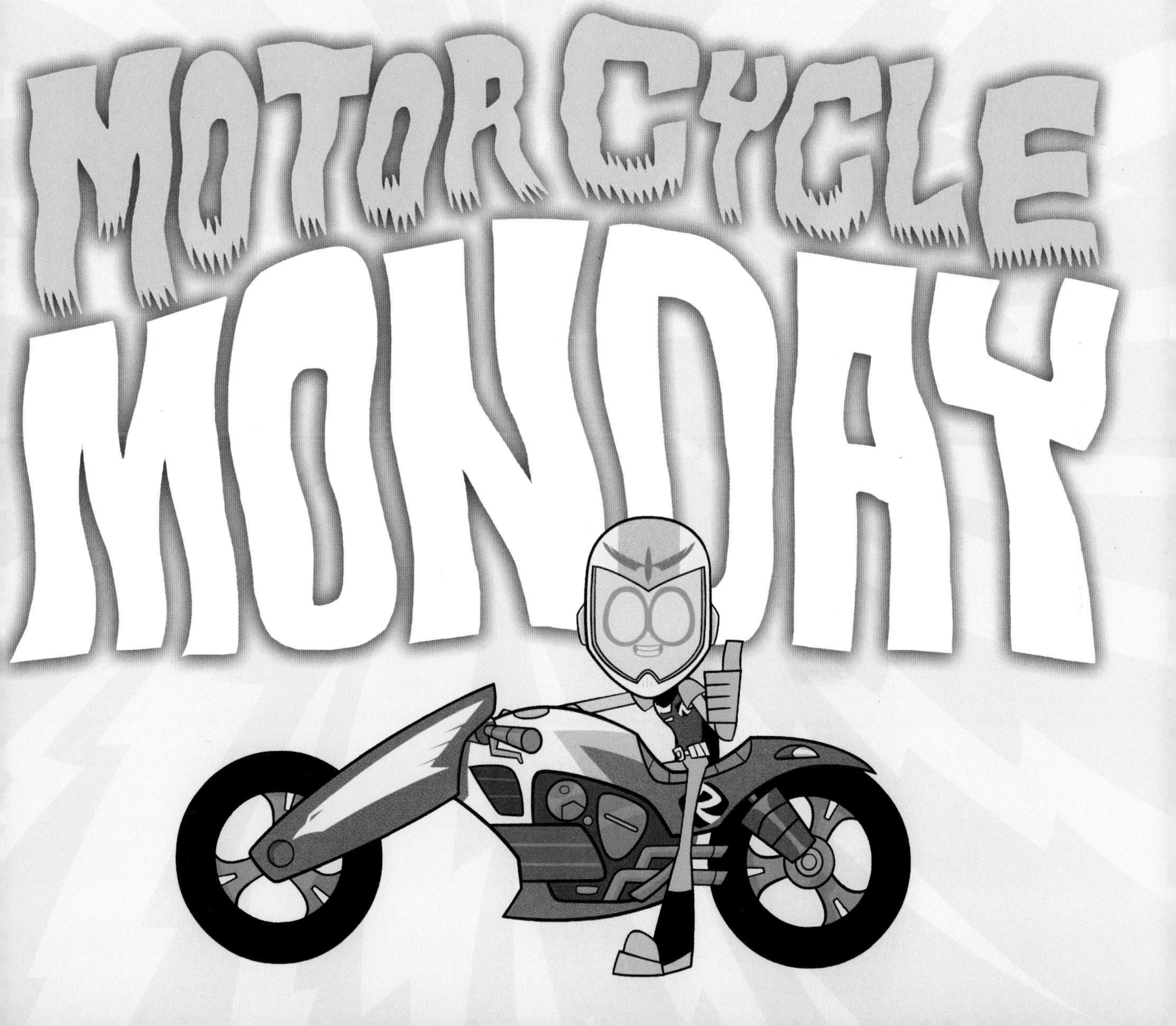
MOTOR CYCLE
MONDAY

"Uhhh, Motorcycle Monday?" Raven asks.

Cyborg rolls his eyes and explains, "Robin says on Mondays we're only allowed to use motorcycles to fight bad guys."

"But he knows we do not possess such modes of transportation!" Starfire decries.

"So *convenient*, isn't it?" Beast Boy snorts.

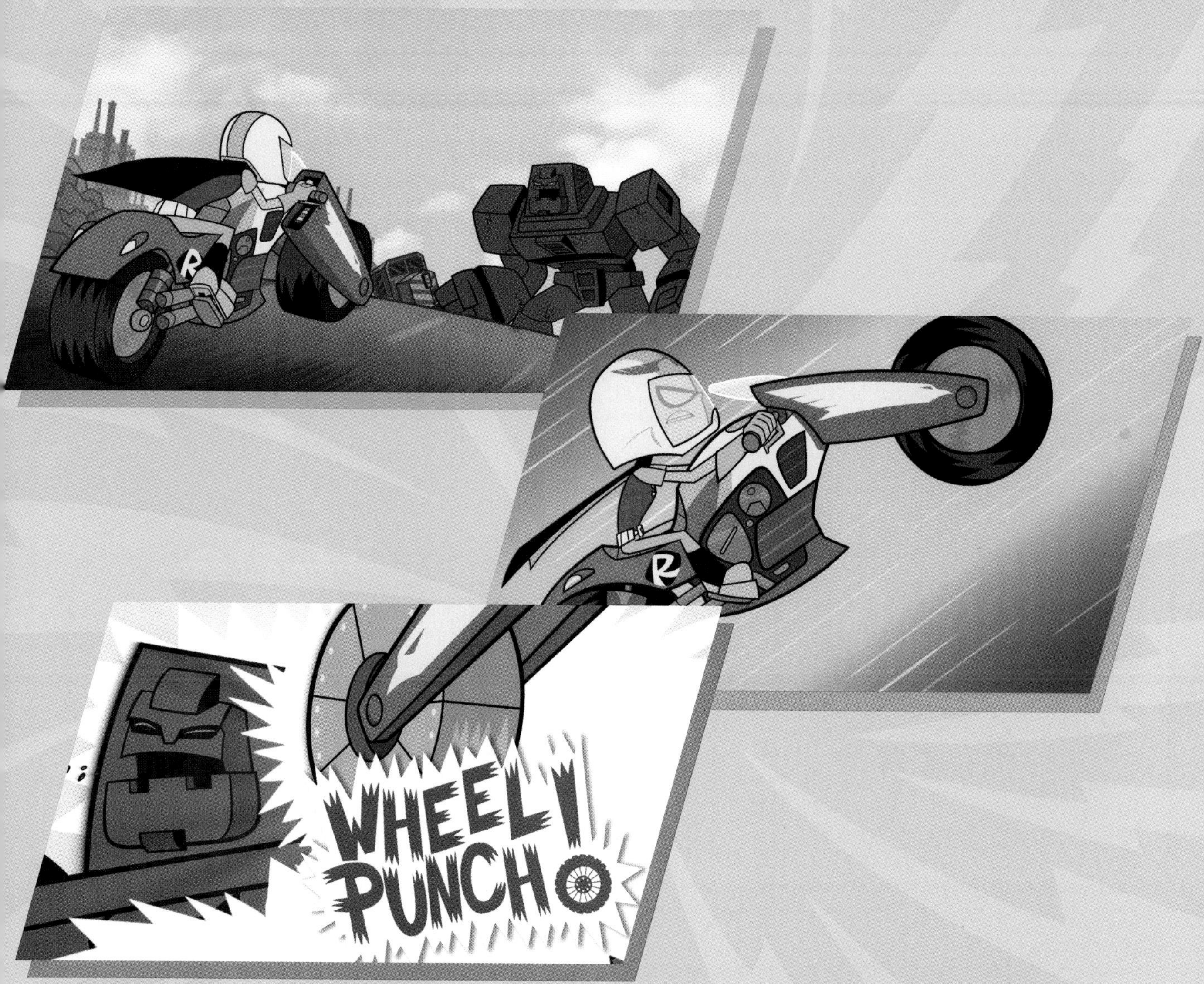
WHEEL PUNCH!

And so it is Robin, the only Teen Titan with a motorcycle, who races toward Cinderblock and delivers a wheel punch!

Cinderblock is no match for Robin's motorbike combat skills!

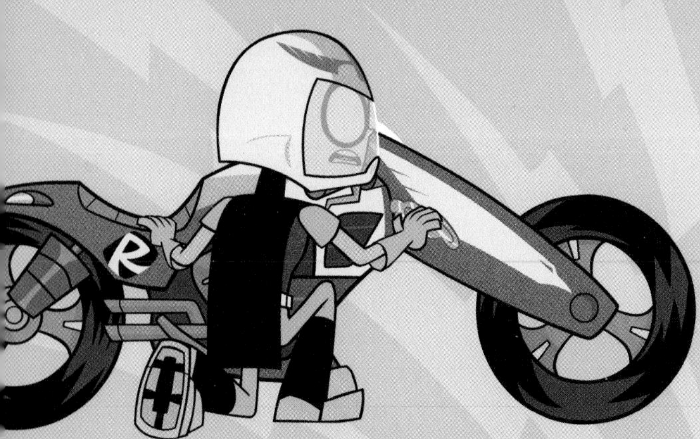

Back at Titans Tower, Robin polishes his precious cycle while gloating about his victory.

"I am the greatest super hero *ever*!" he proclaims.

"No, you're not," Raven disagrees.

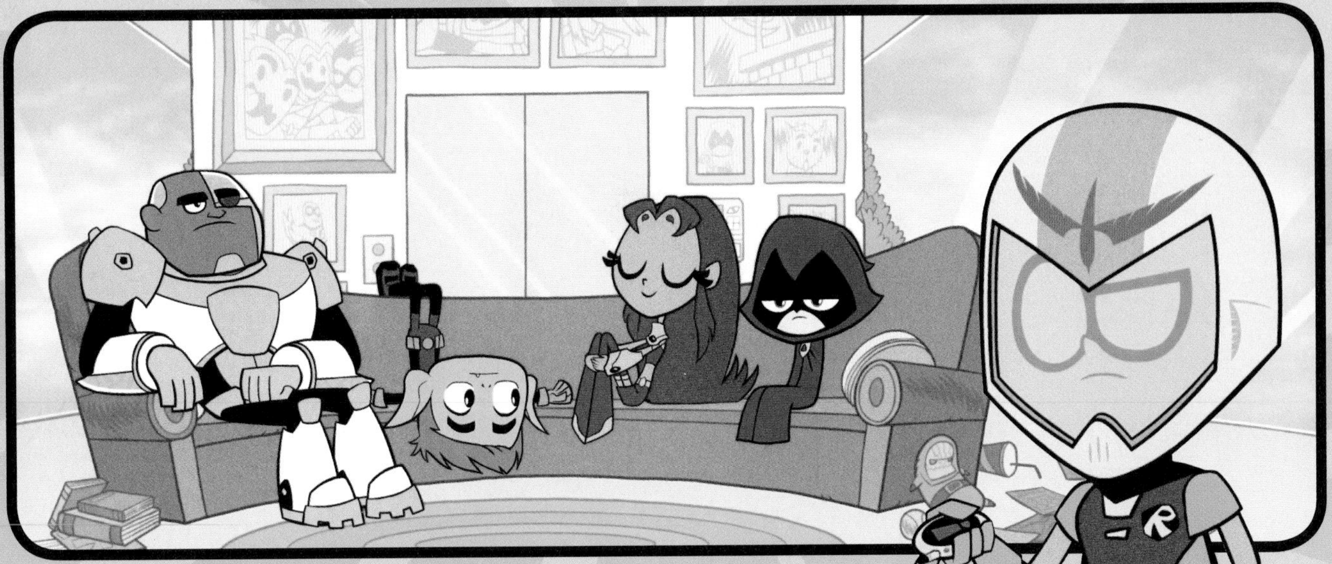

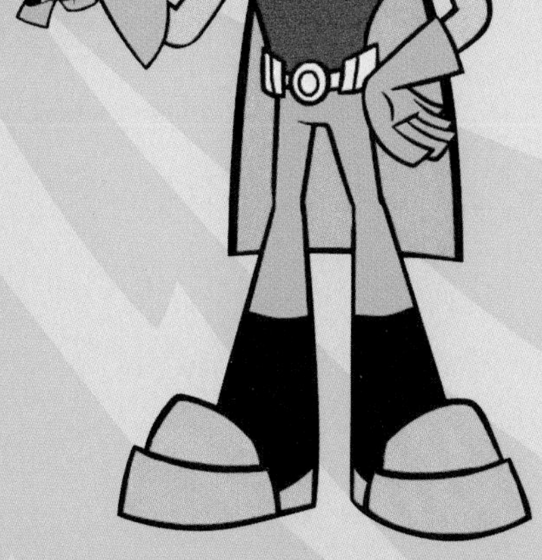

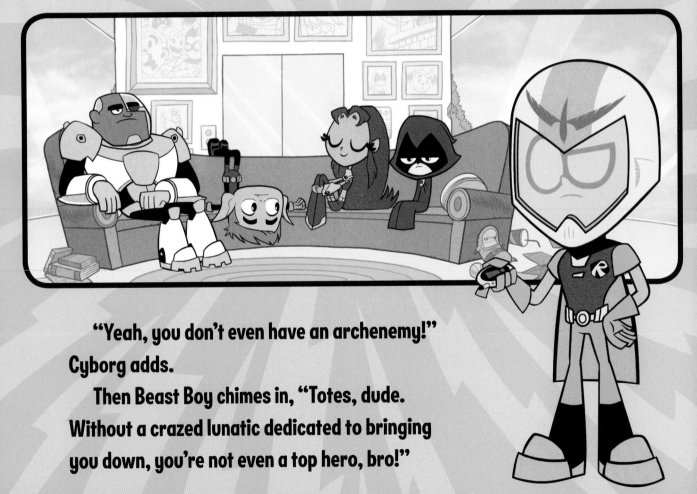

"Yeah, you don't even have an archenemy!" Cyborg adds.

Then Beast Boy chimes in, "Totes, dude. Without a crazed lunatic dedicated to bringing you down, you're not even a top hero, bro!"

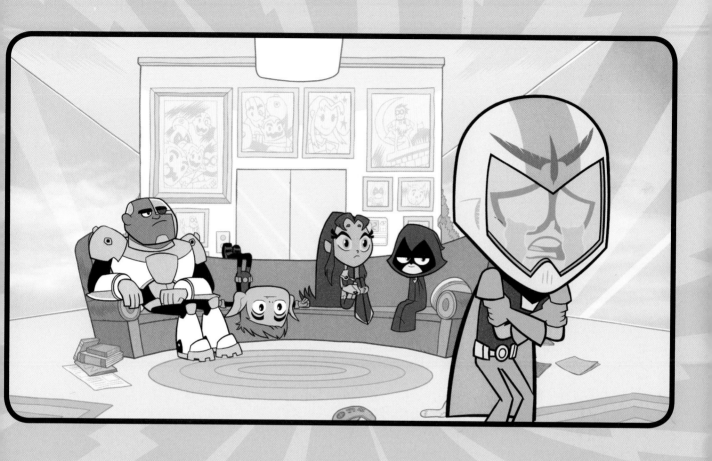

Robin tries to stay strong, but he realizes he actually
does not have an archnemesis of his own. It is crushing.
He breaks down in a flurry of tears.
 "Why doesn't anyone want to beat me up?" Robin cries.
"Without an archenemy, I'm just a nerd...like you guys!"

Starfire feels awful for Robin. She tries to comfort him. "Oh, Robin, I will be your archenemy!"

"Only villains can be archenemies, Star," Cyborg explains.

"Then I will become a villain! I shall be called *Starfire the Terrible*!" Starfire declares.

Beast Boy laughs and says, "If you're going to be a villain, you've got to prove it. Do something *evil*!"

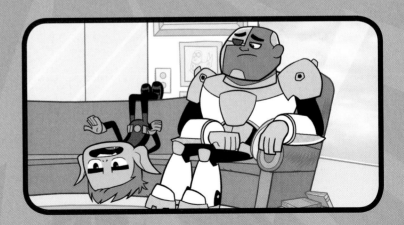

Starfire thinks about evil things for a moment. Then she gets an idea. She flies to the kitchen and returns with...milk.

"Very well. I will do something most evil. I will drink straight from the carton!" Starfire exclaims.

She tries her hardest to do this very diabolical deed, but she can't bring herself to drink without a glass. "I cannot do it. It is *too* evil."

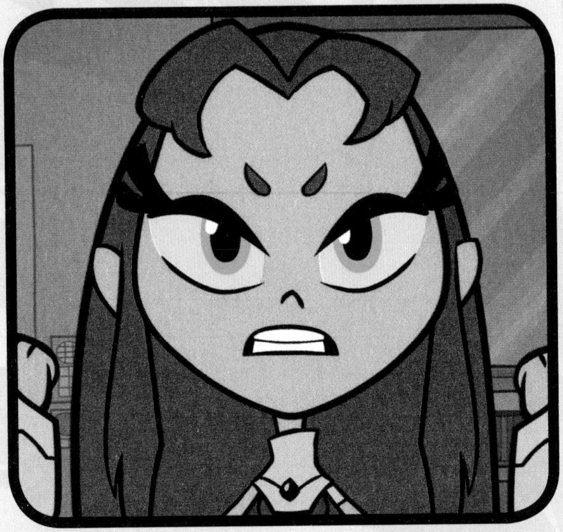

Even though she could not drink milk from the carton, Starfire still vows to wreak havoc on the world—at least until Robin is happy again. She retreats to her bedroom to reinvent herself as a villain.

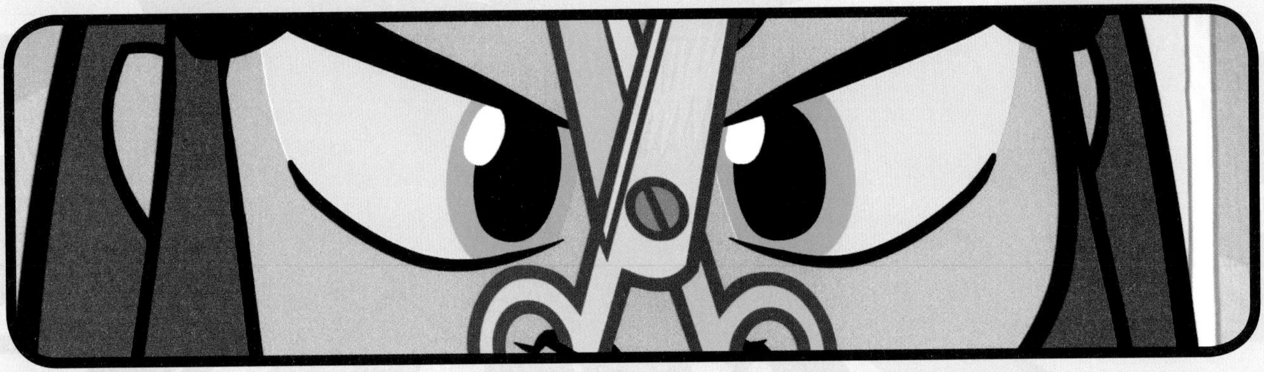

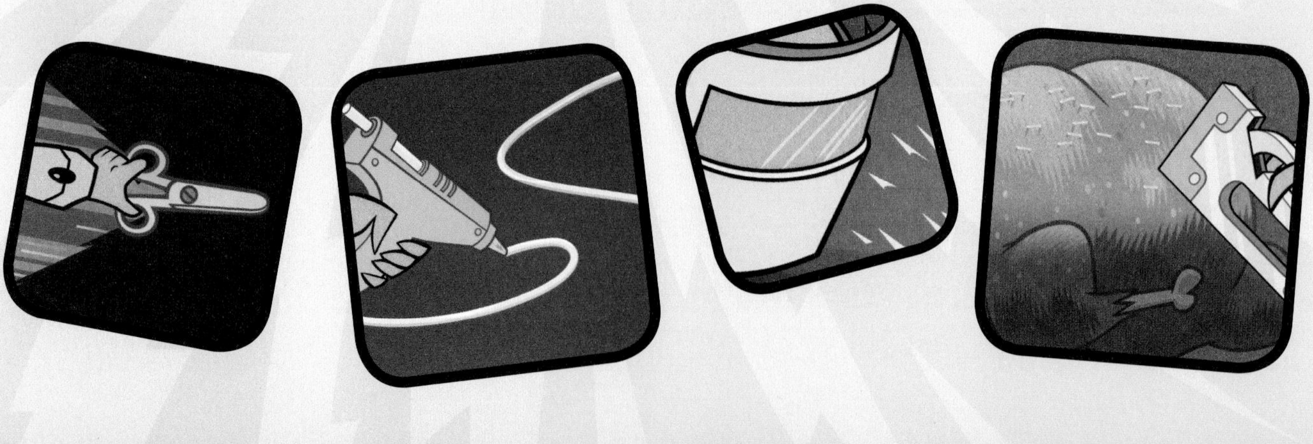

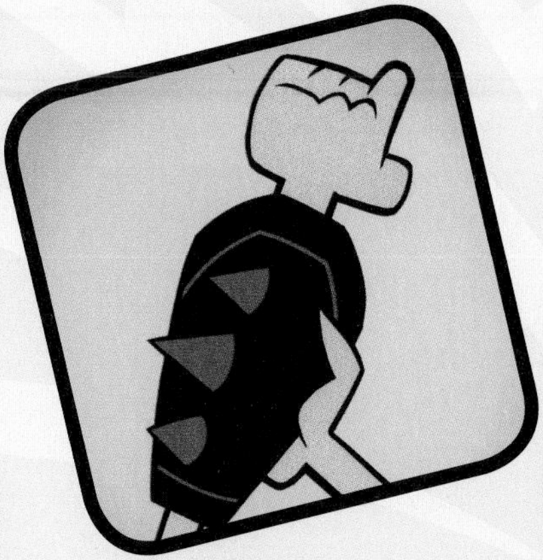

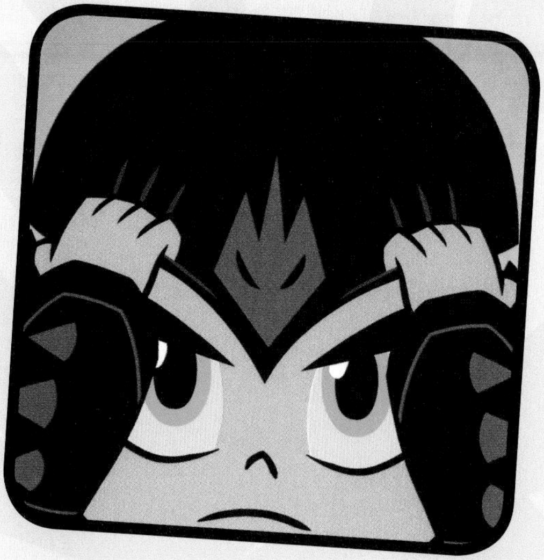

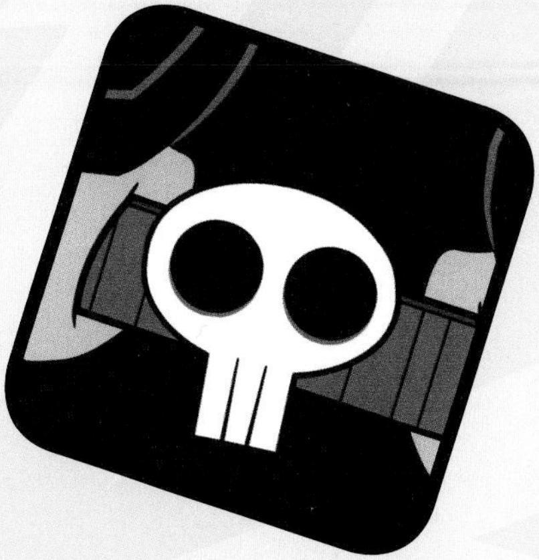

"Robin deserves nothing but the best, so there is much work to be done!" she says.

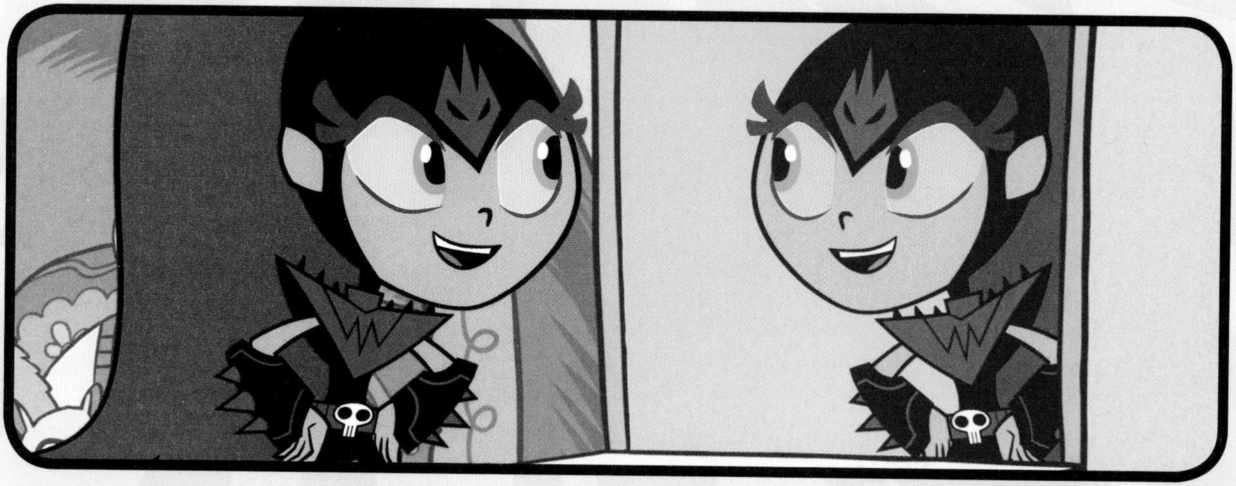

After she finishes her costume, Starfire needs a dangerous henchman and a base of operations to complete her transformation. She employs her wormy pet, Silkie, as her coldhearted sidekick. Together, they build a new secret lair.

"From here I will plunge this world into its darkest days!" Starfire shouts with a very evil laugh. "Ooh, and have tea parties!"

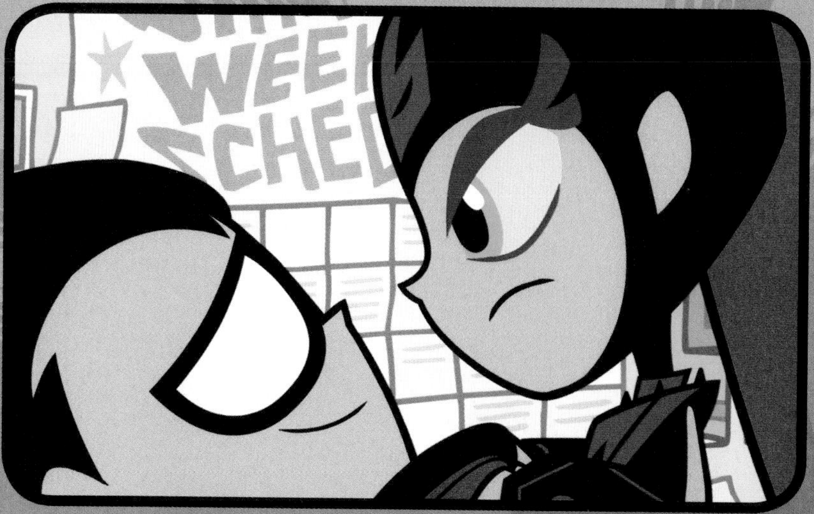

Starfire the Terrible is finally ready to confront her nemesis, Robin. To prove herself as a very menacing foe, Starfire destroys what Robin holds most dear—his precious hair gel! Robin's spiky hair is now flat!

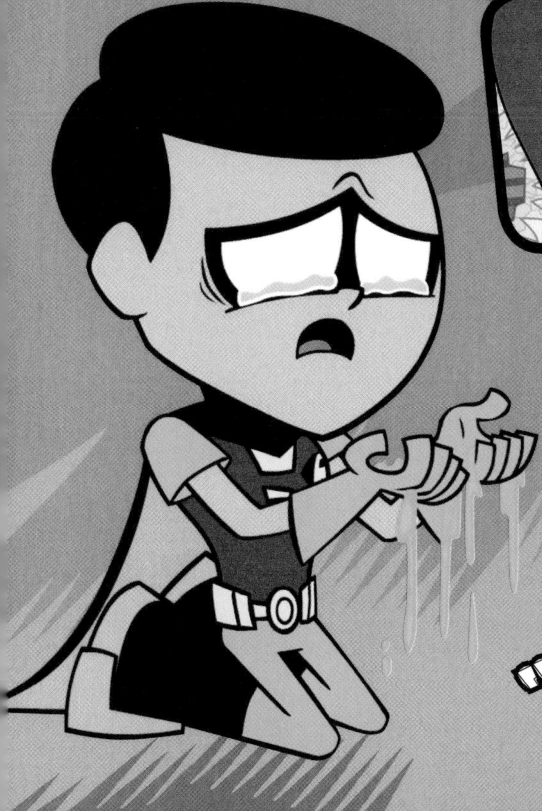

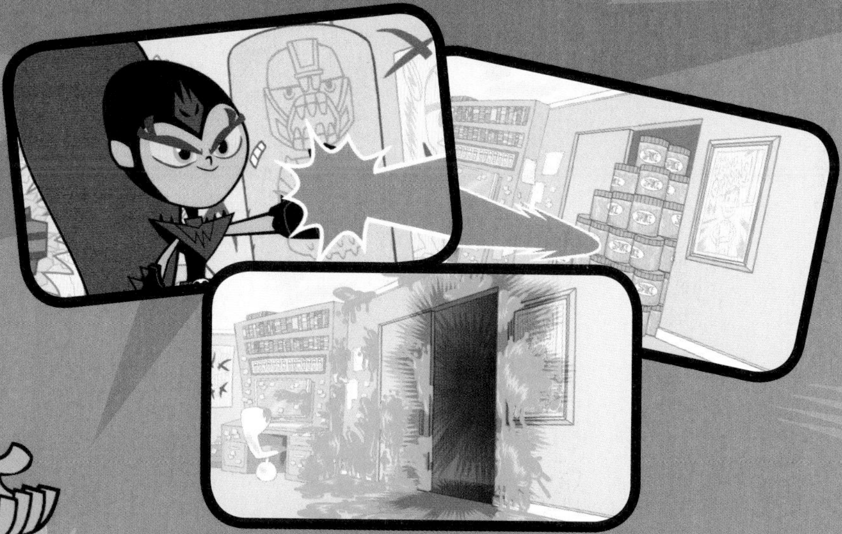

He screams in torment,

"NOOOOOOOOOO!"

Later, Beast Boy, Raven, and Cyborg are playing video games when Robin bursts in and yells, "Titans! My archenemy is on the loose! Starfire...*the Terrible*!"

The Titans all erupt in laughter.

"Come on, man, for real?" Beast Boy giggles.

"Sure. Go ahead. Laugh now. You won't be laughing when you see how nefarious she's become. She blew up my hair gel. *My. Hair. Gel!*"

The Titans laugh even harder.

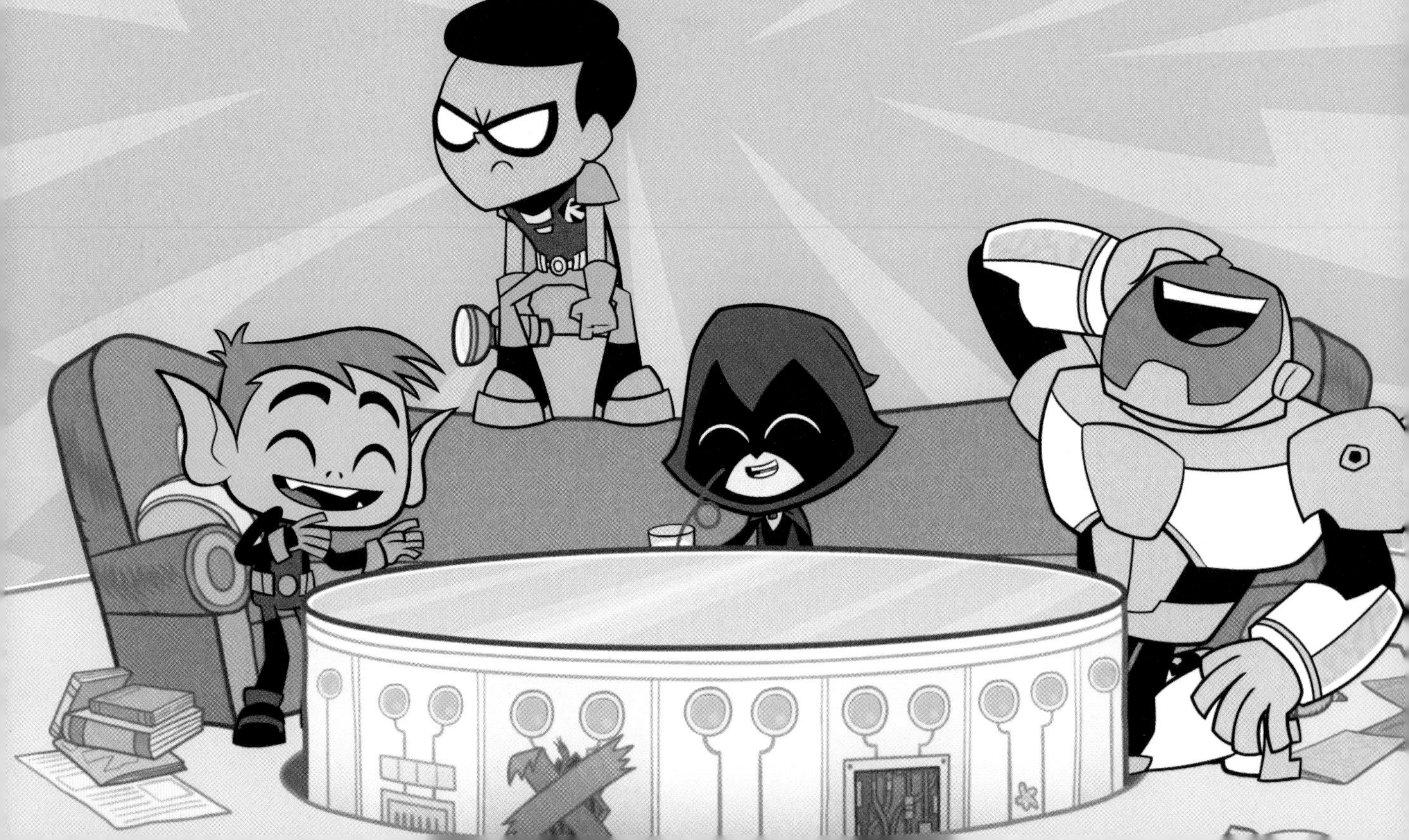

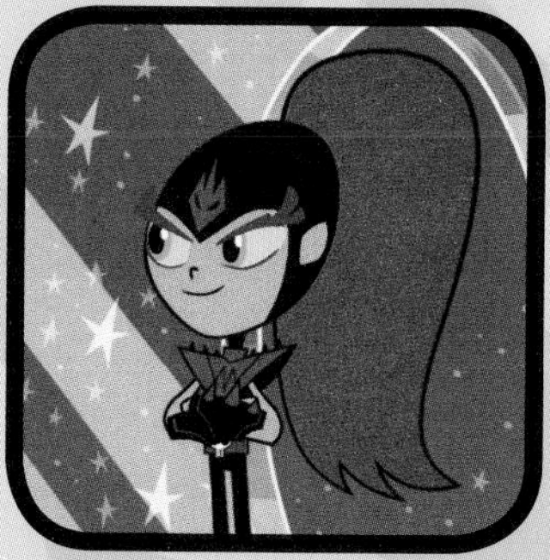

Just then, Starfire the Terrible blasts a hole in the window and makes an entrance! "Greetings, former friends."

Robin is ready to throw down, but the other Titans laugh at her.

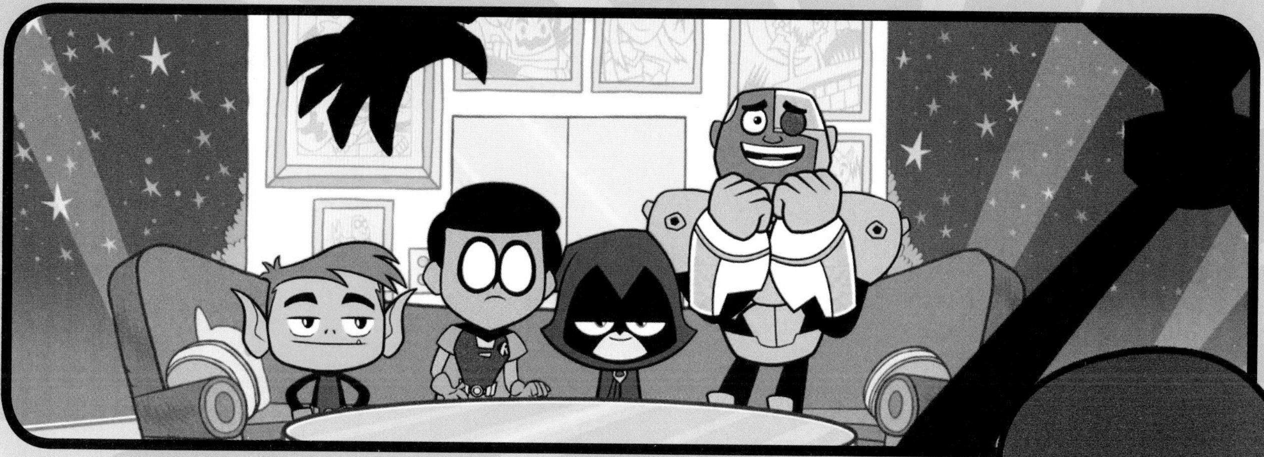

"You will not be laughing when you see that I, Starfire the Terrible, have rigged the moon to explode!" Starfire threatens.

Cyborg snickers. "Star, you couldn't even drink milk from the carton and now you're going to blow up the moon? Riiiiight." The Titans start laughing again, but that's when...

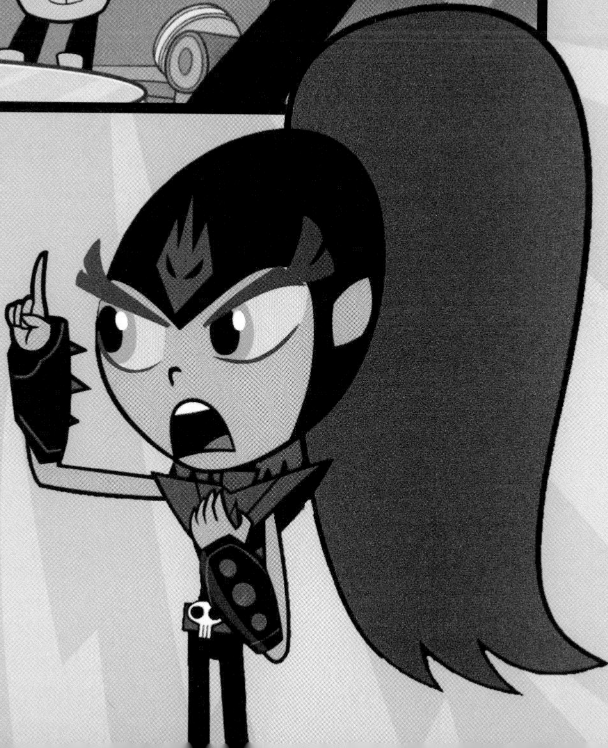

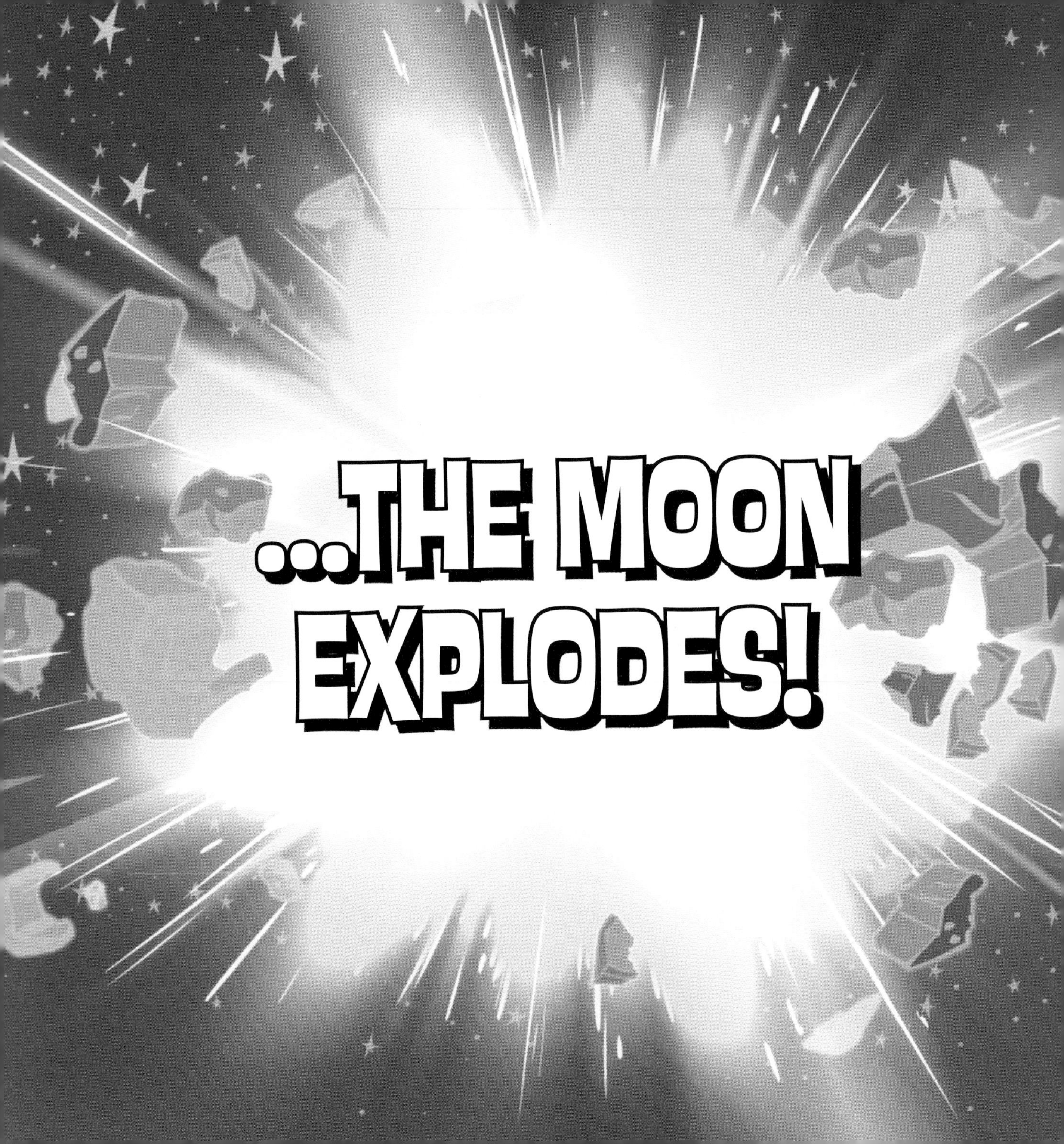
...THE MOON
EXPLODES!

"Did you just blow up *the moon*? Don't you even care about the tides?" Cyborg shouts.

Raven demands, "Why would you do such a thing?"

"Because I know how much Robin likes that moon!" Starfire replies proudly.

Beast Boy screams, "Are you *crazy*, Starfire?"

Starfire answers, "Yes, and the evil, too!" Then she giggles and flies off.

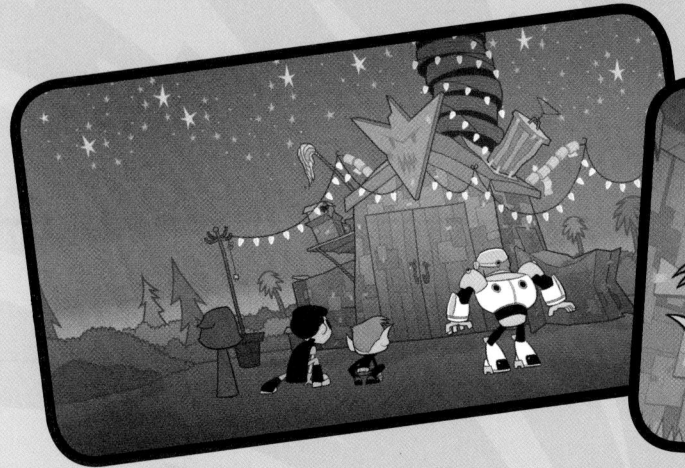

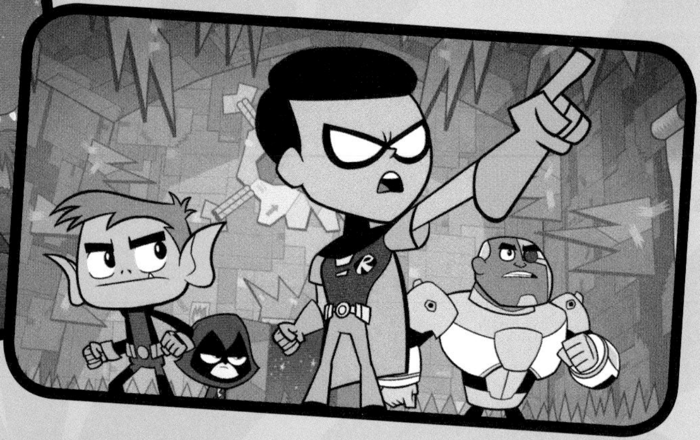

The Teen Titans track Starfire the Terrible back to her headquarters. They barge in through the front door and find her waiting for them.

"I see you have discovered my secret lair," she addresses them as a spider would welcome a fly to its web.

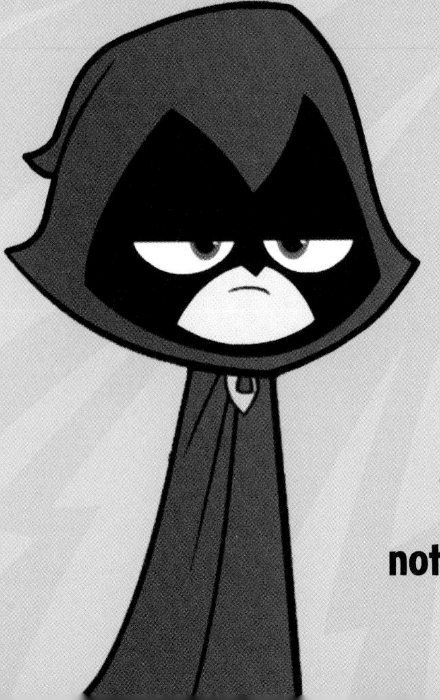

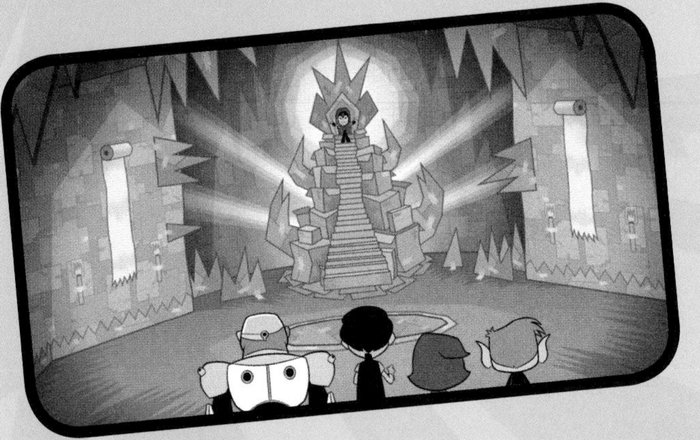

"Uhhh, yeah, well, it's in our backyard, soooo... not really that secret," Raven mutters.

"Your reign of terror is over, Starfire! Titans, go!" Robin commands.

Before the Titans know it, Starfire unleashes her cardboard lasers and merciless deathbots on them.

The Titans put up a valiant fight, but they are no match for Starfire the Terrible's defenses. She proves to be a formidable foe and defeats them without even leaving the throne she is perched on.

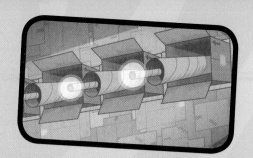

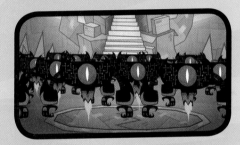

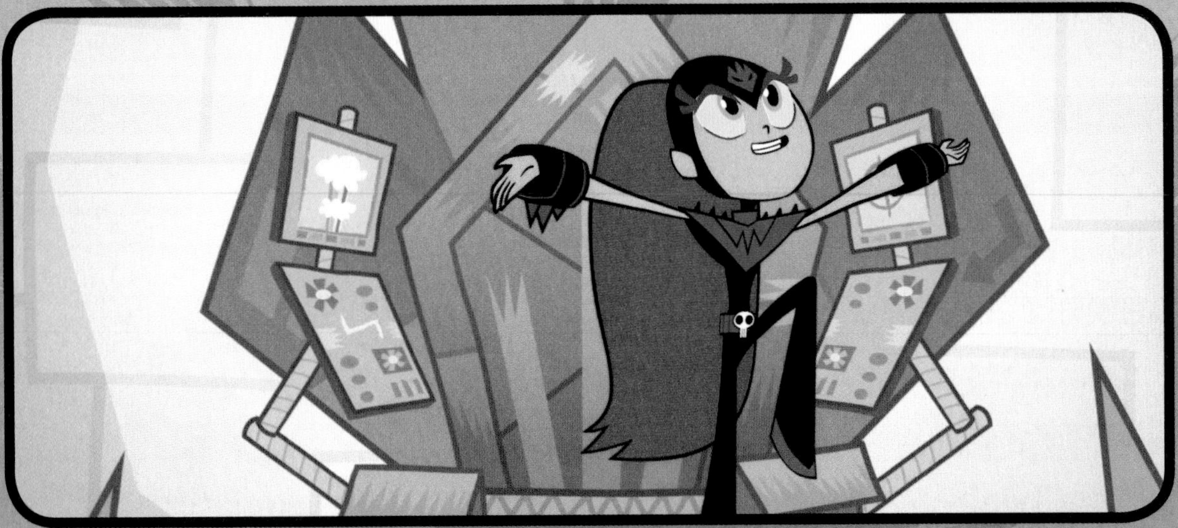

"Hooray! I win! I am afraid I have to finish you now," Starfire exclaims wickedly.

Could this be the end of the Teen Titans' flat-haired leader?

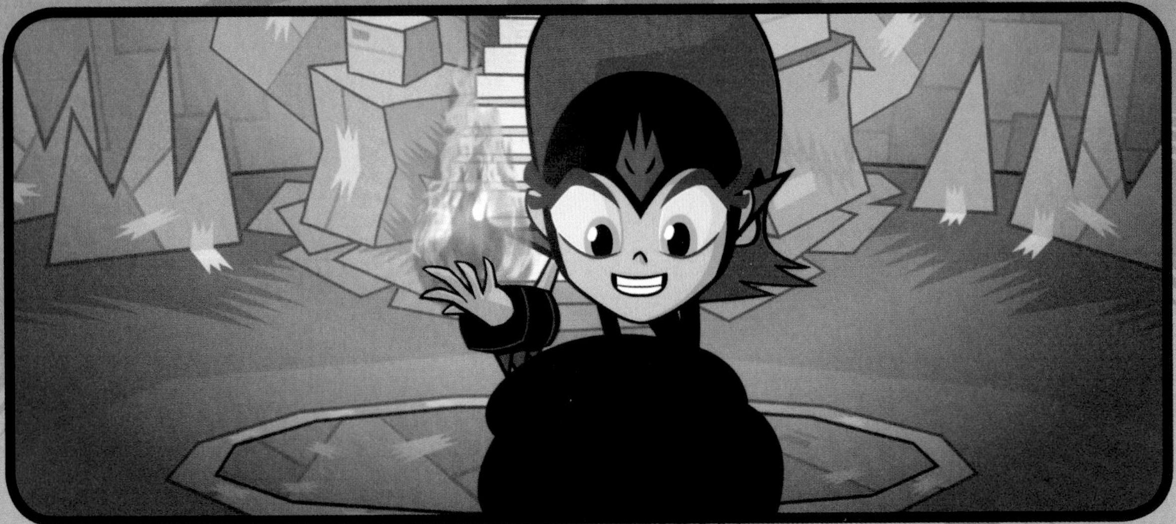

Robin lies on the ground in defeat. He sighs and asks if he can have one last request.

Starfire feels she will not be a very good archenemy if she does not grant him a final wish.

Robin asks, "I was just wondering...what day of the week is it?"

"Hmm. I believe it is the Monday," Starfire replies.

"You know what that means!" Robin smirks and presses a button on his Titan communicator.

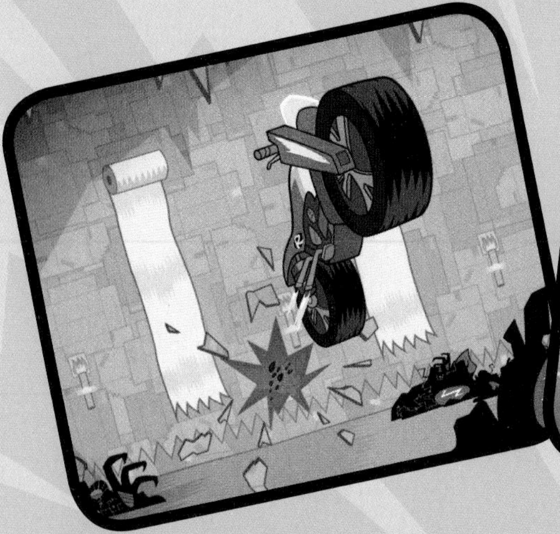

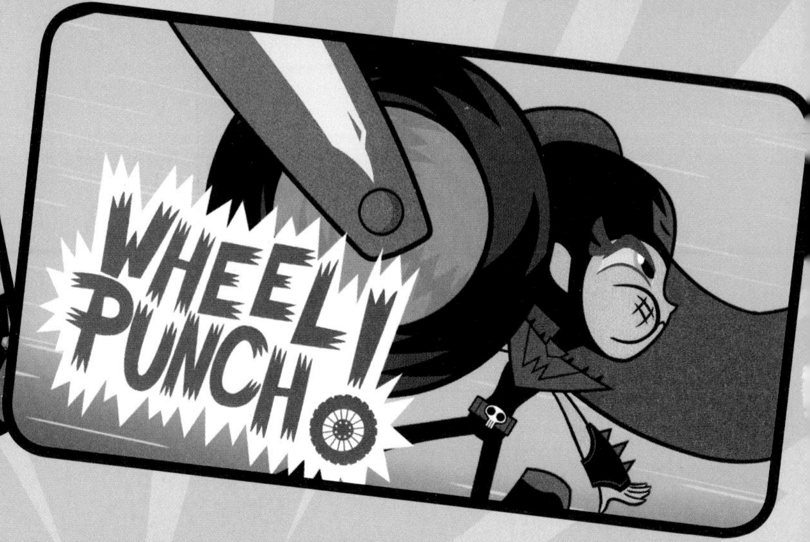
WHEEL PUNCH!

"Wheel punch!" Robin roars as his motorcycle smashes through the wall and right toward Starfire!

"Ha-ha! Gotcha! In your face! I beat my archenemy! Greatest super hero ever!" Robin gloats. Then he shouts, "MOTORRRCYCLLLLE MONDAYYYY!" as he rides off into the night.

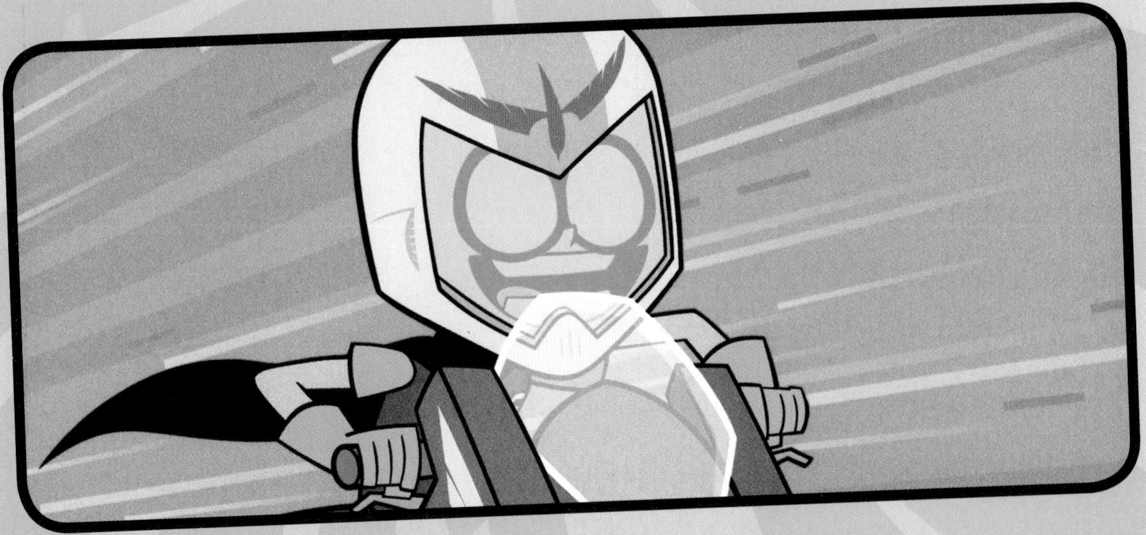